TWO of a kind™
Diaries

Win a
super-cool
electric guitar!
Details on page 99

Look for more

titles:

TWO of a kind™
Diaries
Camp Rock 'n' Roll

by Judy Katschke
from the series created by
Robert Griffard & Howard Adler

HarperEntertainment
An Imprint of HarperCollinsPublishers
A PARACHUTE PRESS BOOK

A PARACHUTE PRESS BOOK

Parachute Publishing, L.L.C.
156 Fifth Avenue
Suite 302
New York, NY 10010

Published by

📕HarperEntertainment

An Imprint of HarperCollins*Publishers*
10 East 53rd Street, New York, NY 10022-5299

TWO OF A KIND books created and produced by
Parachute Publishing, L.L.C., in cooperation with Dualstar Publications,
a division of Dualstar Entertainment Group, LLC,
published by HarperEntertainment, an imprint of HarperCollins Publishers.

ISBN 0-06-059528-0

HarperCollins®,📕 ® , and HarperEntertainment™ are trademarks of
HarperCollins Publishers Inc.

First printing: June 2004

Printed in the United States of America

Visit HarperEntertainment on the World Wide Web at
www.harpercollins.com

10 9 8 7 6 5 4 3 2 1

Chapter 1

Sunday

Dear Diary,

I thought this day would never come! My twin sister, Ashley, and I are finally on the bus going to Camp Rock 'n' Roll, and the bus is already rocking!

A girl with bright orange hair across the aisle is playing a keyboard. Three girls in the back of the bus are singing at the top of their lungs. Other girls are playing guitars, tambourines, and even a fiddle!

Ashley is sitting right in front of me, strumming her acoustic guitar.

"Pump it up, you guys," a curly-haired girl with a trumpet shouted, "so they can hear us all the way at camp!"

You've probably figured out, Diary, that Camp Rock 'n' Roll is not a typical bug-juice-and-sports summer camp. It's a totally cool music camp for middle-school girls.

Going to Camp Rock 'n' Roll this summer was my idea. Ever since I was a little kid I've thought it would be awesome to be in a band. As soon as I showed Ashley the Camp Rock 'n' Roll brochure, she was itching to go, too.

"It says you have to bring a musical instrument to camp or know how to play one," Ashley said back at our boarding school, White Oak Academy for Girls in New Hampshire. Ashley and I are both in the First Form, which is what our school calls the seventh grade. "Hey, I can take our guitar!"

"You mean *your* guitar," I said. "You're the only one who plays it now."

Ashley and I both took guitar lessons a couple of years ago. I quit guitar to take piano lessons. Then I quit piano lessons so I could play softball.

"What instrument will you take?" Ashley asked.

"I'm not," I said. "All I want to do is sing!"

It was a no-brainer, Diary. I've already starred in two musicals at White Oak. I love everything about being onstage—belting out songs, taking bows to all that applause—even the hot stage lights and the crowded dressing room. I'm always totally happy when I'm performing.

I glanced at the girl sitting next to me. She was wearing headphones, and she'd been playing her electric guitar since we left Boston. I couldn't tell whether she was rocking out to the beat of her guitar or the music blaring from her Walkman.

"What are you listening to?" I asked her.

The girl smiled. She was wearing a black T-shirt, ripped-up jeans, and lots of leather jewelry with studs.

"It's Gag Reflex's newest CD, *Regurgitate*," she

said. "Next I'm going to listen to Rodney Beecham's latest disc."

I knew all about Gag Reflex. They're a cool heavy metal band. Rodney Beecham is a superfamous British rock singer. All the radio stations play his tunes.

"I'm Mary-Kate Burke," I said.

"I'm Janelle Chow," she said. "I guess you figured out that I'm a serious metal-head."

I did notice one thing about Janelle's head: Her spiky black hair was full of green streaks.

"Is that stuff permanent?" I asked, pointing to her bright green bangs.

"It washes out," Janelle explained. "This hair dye is made out of vegetables, not chemicals."

As the bus rumbled along the highway toward Pennsylvania, Janelle and I told each other about our schools and families. Janelle is a twin like I am. She has a twin brother named Joshua, whom she says she is *nothing* like. He's a total computer geek.

"Ashley and I look alike but we're different, too," I said. "I like performing, horseback riding, and sports. Ashley likes ballet, writing, and shopping. But we both *love* music."

"Then you'll both *love* Camp Rock 'n' Roll," Janelle said. "It's totally awesome."

"How do you know?" I asked.

"I went there last year," Janelle said. "Where do you think I learned how to do *this*?"

Janelle played a lightning-fast riff on the guitar, then pumped one fist in the air. "That was *without* my amp," she said, smiling. "Wait till you hear me with juice."

Janelle started telling me all about Camp Rock 'n' Roll. "Every day we have music classes and some sporty stuff like volleyball or canoeing. But the best part of camp is the Battle of the Bands. First we're all split into bands. Then each camper has to pick an instrument to play."

"Or sing?" I asked.

"All of us get to sing," Janelle said. She went on. "The bands compete in four different rounds. In the fourth round the two bands with the highest total scores from the first three rounds compete for the title of Best Band."

"Cool!" I said.

"I wonder if Terrence 'the Terror' Boyle will be one of the judges this summer," Janelle said, almost to herself. "He's the only judge who tells it like it is."

That didn't worry me. Honesty is good when you're learning. And I want to learn everything about singing rock.

No more singing in the shower for me, Diary. Next stop, Camp Rock 'n' Roll!

Camp Rock 'n' Roll

Dear Diary,

Sorry for the squiggly writing, but the bus keeps hitting a ton of bumps. And the girl across the aisle keeps hitting me with the neck of her bass guitar!

So far, I *love* Camp Rock 'n' Roll—even though we're not there yet. Mary-Kate is going, and so is my best friend and school roommate, Phoebe Cahill.

Four weeks ago Phoebe's family's summer vacation plans fell through. She went into a real funk.

"What am I going to do all summer?" Phoebe wailed. "I must be the only girl at school with no plans!"

Plans? I suddenly had the perfect plan!

"Phoebe, you should come to Camp Rock 'n' Roll with me," I said. "You play guitar better than I do. And you write the most awesome songs, too."

"I'm not the rock type, Ashley," Phoebe said. "I like singing serious songs with messages. Like Jewel and Sheryl Crow. And some of the folksingers of the sixties."

I smiled at Phoebe sitting cross-legged on her bed in her tie-dyed tee and bell-bottoms. Not only did she listen to the singers of the sixties, she dressed like them, too.

No surprise there. Phoebe's closet at school is

packed with vintage clothes from antique boutiques and flea markets. It's what makes Phoebe . . . Phoebe.

"Don't worry," I said. "I'm sure you can play whatever kinds of songs you want at Camp Rock 'n' Roll."

"Well . . ." Phoebe said slowly, "I don't know."

Diary, when I get an idea, I don't give up easily.

"Please, please, please come to camp with me, Phoebe!" I plopped down on the bed next to her. "We'll have so much fun playing our guitars and coming up with songs!"

"I'll think about it," Phoebe said.

I had to make Phoebe go with me. So I put pictures of Camp Rock 'n' Roll all over our dorm room. I whispered "Camp Rock 'n' Roll" into Phoebe's ear while she slept. I wrote Camp Rock 'n' Roll with the pepperoni on our pizza!

I wanted Phoebe to come to camp more than anything because she's like a second sister to me. We share secrets, a room at school, and—if Phoebe didn't have such a unique style—we'd share clothes. I knew I'd miss her like crazy if I had to go to camp without her.

As summer drew closer, Phoebe still couldn't decide. "What if I don't make any friends at camp?" she asked. "What if all the girls are the bubblegum-pop type? You know I don't click with them."

"Don't worry," I assured her. "I promise we'll stick together all through camp, no matter what."

"Promise?" Phoebe asked.

I drew an imaginary X on my chest and said, "Cross my heart and hope to croak. Drop an eyeball in my Coke."

"Okay," Phoebe said. "But remember: I'm going to sing thoughtful music—not that glitter and midriff stuff."

But on the bus to camp, Phoebe started to worry again.

"Ashley," she whispered. "Look at all the girls going to camp. They're all dressed so . . . so . . . trendy."

I looked around. The girl playing bass guitar had on a floor-length denim skirt and a camouflage tank. One girl's jacket had the word SUPERSTAR written on the back with silver studs. The girl sitting next to Mary-Kate had green hair!

I studied Phoebe in her simple white peasant blouse and faded vintage jeans. "Musicians don't have to dress a certain way," I said. "We'll have fun no matter what."

Phoebe started strumming her guitar. I was about to join in with my own when Mary-Kate tapped my shoulder.

"Ashley," she said. "I think we're here!"

I leaned over Phoebe and stared out the window.

The bus passed through a gate decorated with music notes.

A bunch of college-age kids cheered the bus as it rolled onto the campgrounds. Some wore tees with the word COUNSELOR. Others had tees that read ROADIE. I knew from going to concerts that roadies set up the musical instruments and amps for their favorite bands.

The counselors and roadies circled the bus as it hissed to a stop. Then they all started to play *kazoos*!

"This *is* going to be fun!" Phoebe giggled.

I glanced back at Mary-Kate, and she gave me a big thumbs-up sign. We were at Camp Rock 'n' Roll at last!

Chapter 2

Later Sunday

Dear Diary,

I know I already wrote you today, but I just *have* to tell you about my first day at Camp Rock 'n' Roll!

Everything about this place is cool. There's a main house and five bunks. Behind the bunks is a field for sports. (Not that you'll find *me* there, Diary.) Farther down a hill is an awesome lake for swimming, canoeing, and kayaking. The camp has its own theater, and a music building for classes and practice. There's an arts and crafts hut and a rec hall, and a mess hall for eating meals.

Here's the best part so far: Mary-Kate, Phoebe, and I are all in the same bunk.

"See?" I told Phoebe. "I told you we'd all get to be together."

Mary-Kate and I have been to lots of summer camps before, and the bunks are usually named after birds or bugs. Not at Camp Rock 'n' Roll. Here, the bunks are named after rock superstars. Ours is named Bunk Elvis.

"Elvis Presley was called the King of Rock 'n' Roll," Mary-Kate said. "So *that* means Bunk Elvis totally rules!"

Aside from the painting of Elvis on the door, our bunk looks like any other camp bunk. We have three sets of bunk beds, and each of us has her own cubby. There are two closets—one for clothes and one for musical instruments—plus a bathroom with the skinniest shower stall I ever saw.

The one single bed is for our counselor, Ivy Loomis. Ivy is a college music major and wears lots of bracelets and colorful beads in her cornrows.

Our two other bunk mates are Janelle Chow and Lark Maitland. Lark has long dark hair and big sad-looking brown eyes. Janelle is her total opposite. She has a huge smile that's about as electric as her guitar.

"Yo, dudes!" Janelle shouted, waving her guitar in the air. "Who's ready for some monster rock?"

"Not me," Phoebe murmured.

We dropped our duffel bags and instruments on the floor. I noticed one of the beds was empty.

"There's one more girl coming who didn't take the bus," Ivy explained. "Her name is Erin Verko."

"Did someone say my name?" a perky voice asked.

I spun around. A girl with long pin-straight blond hair bounced into the bunk. She was wearing a pink halter top and black cropped pants decorated with silver zippers.

"You guys!" Erin said with a little jump. "Is music camp going to be superfun or what?"

I stared at Erin. With her cutting-edge clothes, she looked as if she had stepped right out of a fashion magazine!

"Where's your gear, Erin?" Ivy asked.

Just then three roadies entered the bunk. Two of the guys lugged duffel bags and wheeled suitcases. The third carried a long black case.

"What is all *that*?" Phoebe asked.

"Just my keyboard case," Erin said. She began to pull clothes out of a suitcase. "And a few things to wear."

"A few?" Janelle echoed. "No wonder you didn't take the bus—there wasn't enough room!"

"Exactly." Erin giggled as the guys left the bunk. I couldn't take my eyes off Erin's clothing. That's because all my life I've had a serious passion for fashion. Now, right in my own bunk, was a fellow style-freak!

"Erin, your clothes are awesome. Where do you go shopping?" I just had to ask.

"I don't. My mom's the fashion editor for *Teen Scene* magazine," Erin explained. "She gets a lot of the clothes they use in the photo shoots."

"I love *Teen Scene*!" I said. I checked out some of the clothes on the bed. "Omigosh—these pants were on the cover of the May issue. And this jacket was in the 'Gotta Have It!' section of the April issue!"

"Dead on!" Erin said. She looked me up and down. "You look like you're about my size. You can borrow some of my clothes, if you want."

"No way!" I squealed.

"Yes, way!" Erin squealed back.

"I'm Ashley, by the way," I added.

"Shut *up*!" Erin cried. "My *middle* name is Ashley!"

"No way!" I cried.

"Start unpacking, girls," Ivy said. "There's a campfire jam tonight. You'll get to sing, play your instruments, and meet the Battle of the Bands judges."

We all chatted and laughed as we unpacked and made our beds. Only Lark didn't say much, but she grinned when Mary-Kate spread out her Chicago Cubs sheets. Phoebe made her bed like she does at school, with Indian paisley throws. I was tucking in my turquoise sheets when I heard a loud puffing noise. I turned around. Erin was sitting cross-legged on the floor, blowing up something plastic and pink.

"What's that?" I asked.

"It's my inflatable chair," Erin said. "Just because we're in the woods at camp doesn't mean we have to rough it, right?"

"Right," I agreed. I'd always wanted a chair like that for my room at school.

Erin gazed around the bunk. "Now where should I hang up my beaded curtain . . . and plug in my karaoke machine?"

I could see Phoebe roll her eyes behind her blue-frame glasses. "Erin Verko is like a breakfast cereal," she whispered to me. "Flaky!"

"You're wrong," I whispered back to Phoebe. "I think she's fun!"

Dear Diary,

Wait until you hear about the amazing campfire I just went to. Everyone showed up with an instrument. There was every kind—from a violin to drums. The only campers without instruments were Lark and me.

"Do you play an instrument, Lark?" I asked.

Lark shook her head and said, "I kind of sing."

"Really?" I said. "Me too."

Lark dropped her marshmallow as she was about to put it on her stick. She started to reach for a new one, when a counselor hurried over.

"Take this, Lark," the counselor said. She held out a crispy marshmallow on a stick. "It's already toasted."

Lark's face turned red. "No, thanks," she said.

The counselor looked disappointed as she walked away. I didn't get it. Why was she so eager to give Lark an already-toasted marshmallow? I was about to drop my own marshmallow to see if the same thing would happen, when—

"Welcome to Camp Rock 'n' Roll!" a voice shouted.

A woman wearing black jeans and a red tee was standing on a tree stump. I knew from her picture in the brochure that she was Stella Vickers, the camp owner. Stella used to sing with a group called Heartstrings in the late seventies.

Stella told us about the activities, then about the Battle of the Bands. "Each bunk will be split into two bands. And each band will have one lead vocalist."

That's got to be me! I thought.

"Tomorrow you'll meet your music instructors," Stella went on. "But right now I'd like you to meet our three judges, starting with the one and only Clarence Meekins!"

A tall thin guy wearing a backward baseball cap jumped up. Everyone cheered as he waved both arms.

"Next, the incredibly glam Sophie Amir!" Stella shouted. "Give it up for her, ladies!"

Sophie stood up and waved shyly as everyone cheered. She did look glam in a gold halter top and denim capris.

"And here's the guy who cannot tell a lie," Stella said. "Put your hands together for Terrence Boyle!"

A man with dark curly hair stood up. He rolled his eyes as a few kids hissed and booed. Then everyone laughed.

"Now put down your marshmallows and pick up your instruments!" Stella declared. She picked up her own guitar. "Let's kick off the night with 'Wild Thing.' If you know it, jump in. If you don't, jump in, anyway!"

The campfire crackled as we all jammed. Ashley and Phoebe strummed their guitars. Janelle leaned way back as she played some serious guitar riffs. Erin worked her keyboard, and I sang at the top of my lungs.

Every time I looked at Lark, her mouth was shut. *That's weird*, I thought. *Why doesn't she want to sing?*

We sang and played until the campfire finally fizzled out. Then Stella shouted, "You ladies have it rockin' on. Have a great night and I'll see you all tomorrow!"

Back in Bunk Elvis, Ivy switched on the light and said, "Whoa! Some lucky camper got a care package." She pointed to a large cardboard box that was sitting on Lark's bed. The return address was London, England.

"Who lives in England?" Phoebe asked.

"Just my dad," Lark answered in a small voice.

"Maybe he sent you some English toffees," I said.

"Or English biscuits," Ashley guessed.

"Or Prince William!" Erin teased.

Lark opened the box. It was filled with sweet-smelling soaps, chocolates, and a stack of top-ten CDs.

"*That's* what I call a care package!" Janelle said. "All I ever get from my folks are pretzels and socks."

Lark read the note to herself. Erin peeked over her shoulder and read it out loud: "'Lark—have a super time at camp. Love, Dad.'"

"Can I have that note, Lark?" Ivy asked. "It would be like having an autograph from—"

"It's yours," Lark cut in. Her face turned red again.

We stared at Lark as she gave Ivy the note. Then she ran into the bathroom. What was *that* all about?

Chapter 3

Monday

Dear Diary,

First thing this morning we went to the mess hall for breakfast. Each bunk has its own table. I sat between Phoebe and Mary-Kate. Erin sat right across from me. She kept staring at Phoebe's white blouse with black spirals.

"What's the matter?" Phoebe finally asked Erin. She looked down at her blouse. "Do I have a stain somewhere?"

"No," Erin said. "My mom used to have a blouse like that. She gave it to Goodwill. Maybe it's the same one."

Uh-oh, I thought. *Wrong answer!*

"This is a vintage blouse from nineteen sixty-five," Phoebe told Erin. "I got it at Classique Boutique, not Goodwill."

"I like vintage clothes, too," Erin said. "Especially around Halloween when I want a goofy costume—"

"Waffles anyone?" I cut in.

After breakfast we collected our instruments and followed Ivy to the camp theater.

Stella stood on the stage. "This morning we'll break up into bands," she announced as she studied a clipboard.

Phoebe stood next to me and crossed her fingers. "Please, oh, please let us be in the same one!" she whispered.

"Bunk Elvis," Stella began. "The first band will be Janelle Chow, Mary-Kate Burke, and Lark Maitland. Second band: Ashley Burke, Phoebe Cahill, and Erin Verko."

Phoebe and I let out excited little shrieks. Erin ran over to us, and we all slapped hands and jumped up and down.

After the other bands were announced, each band met their instructor. Ours was Jennifer Stanley. She had long curly black hair and a tee that read GUITAR GODDESS.

"I see we have two acoustic guitarists and a keyboard player," Jennifer said as she checked out our instruments. "What type of band would you like to be?"

"I'd like our band to be called the Songbirds," Phoebe said, her eyes shining. "And we should sing about things that are really important to kids and teens."

"Huh?" Erin said, wrinkling her nose.

"You know," Phoebe explained, "caring for the earth, being true to yourself. Our songs should have meaning."

"I don't think so," Erin said. She frowned, then

snapped her fingers. "Hey, I know. Why don't we call our band something like Teen Spirit?"

"Teen Spirit," I repeated. "That name is so cool!"

"And we should sing about all kinds of fun stuff," Erin went on. "You know—boys, friends, summertime."

Diary, it was like Erin was reading my mind. Summer is my favorite season of the year. It's all about kicking back and having fun. So why not sing about it?

"What do you think?" Erin asked me.

"Are you kidding?" I exclaimed. "We love it!"

"Really?" Erin said with a little jump.

"Totally!" I replied.

"Okay, campers—I mean, rockers!" Stella called out. "Tomorrow morning you'll meet with your instructors for your first band workshop."

Erin grabbed my arm as we walked out of the theater.

"I brought some of that fake tanning spray," she said. "Maybe we can all use it when we sing about summer!"

"That's perfect!" I said.

Diary, I am so incredibly psyched. I'm in the hippest band at camp with my best friend and a cool *new* friend.

Can things get any better than that?

Two of a Kind Diaries

Dear Diary,

Here's the scoop. Janelle and I are in the same band. So is Lark, which is why I'm kind of bummed out.

It all started when we met our instructor, Bill West. Bill has stringy longish hair and wire-rimmed glasses. He had us sit in a circle on the grass.

"Let's talk about your goals for the band," Bill began. "How do you all see yourselves?"

"Totally in leather!" Janelle answered. "We should jump up and down on our instruments when we're finished playing and bite the heads off of chocolate bunnies!"

"Are you serious?" I asked.

"Just about the leather part," Janelle said, giggling.

"Bill?" I said and glanced at Lark. "Can our band have two singers? I want to sing. And I think Lark does, too."

Bill smiled at Lark, ignoring me. "Really, Lark?" he asked. "Do you want to sing?"

"I guess," Lark said with a shrug. She didn't look very excited. Then again, she never did.

"So we'll both sing, right?" I asked Bill.

"Sorry, Mary-Kate," Bill said. "Each band can only have one lead singer. Hey, Stella!" he yelled across the field. "It's a go! Lark is going to sing lead!"

"All-riiiight!" Stella shouted back to him.

Am I missing something? I wondered. *Lark didn't even sing at the campfire. And now she's going to sing lead?*

I looked at Lark. She was inspecting a blade of grass.

"Bill?" I said in a low voice. "Could I speak to you, please? In private?"

"Sure thing," Bill said, still smiling at Lark.

The two of us walked over to a nearby tree. "I was kind of hoping I'd get to sing," I told him. "I starred in my school musicals. I played Kim in *Bye Bye Birdie*, and I—"

"Don't worry," Bill said. "You'll definitely get to sing backup. But Stella really wants Lark to sing solo."

"Why?" I asked.

"You know how it is," Bill said with a shrug.

I *don't* know how it is, Diary. What was going on?

"Can't Lark play an instrument?" I asked. "We all had to write one down on the camp application."

"It's cool," Bill said. "We'll just give Lark a tambourine she can shake around."

I didn't get it. What was the big deal about Lark?

"Speaking of instruments, Mary-Kate," Bill said, "you wrote on your application that you play the piano. Check?"

My eyes flew wide open. Piano? I took my last piano lesson when I was ten years old. When I checked it off on the form, I never thought they'd actually make me play it.

"I did take lessons," I said slowly. "And I can read music."

"Cool!" Bill said. "We'll get you a keyboard tomorrow, and you can start jamming."

"A keyboard?" I echoed.

"It'll be perfect for the band," Bill said. "If you play piano, you'll be able to ace the keyboard in no time."

"C-c-cool," I stammered.

But it really wasn't.

I still wanted to sing lead. And how could I tell Bill that the only song I'd learned to play on the piano was "Itsy Bitsy Spider"?

Chapter 4

Tuesday

Dear Diary,
    Last night in the rec hall the three of us got busy coming up with a name for our band.

    "Okay," Janelle said, looking down at her notepad. "So far we've got The Diva Dollz, In Your Face, and Hangnail. Which one will it be?"

    I thought about each name. Hangnail sounded painful. And In Your Face made us sound too tough. So—

    "The Diva Dollz!" Lark and I said at the same time. We looked at each other and grinned.

    "Diva Dollz," Janelle repeated. "It's a little girly-girl . . . but I think I like it."

    So, Diary, we're The Diva Dollz.

    Our first band practice in the music building came right after breakfast. Janelle, Lark, and I met Bill in Room #5. The room was packed with counselors. I even saw our counselor, Ivy, in a corner.

    "Why are all the counselors here?" I whispered to Janelle.

    "They're probably here to see Lark," Janelle whispered back.

    I was about to ask why, when Bill walked over.

    "I got you a keyboard, Mary-Kate," Bill said. He

pointed to a shiny red keyboard on the side of the room.

"Great!" I said. Would I remember *anything* from those piano lessons? Feeling a little sick, I went over to the keyboard to check it out.

"Janelle, you can plug in your guitar in the corner amp," Bill explained. "Lark, stand behind this microphone. Is it the right level?" He adjusted the stand. "Or is this better?" he asked, adjusting it again.

"Anything is fine," Lark said.

Bill handed Lark a silver tambourine. She gave it a little shake. The counselors went wild.

"Work it, Lark!"

"You got it rockin', girl!"

This is so weird! I thought. *The whole camp is treating Lark as if she's the best thing since Velcro!*

I stood behind the keyboard and tapped on a few keys. There was no sound.

"You forgot to turn it on," Janelle whispered.

"Whoops," I said, flicking the on switch.

"We'll start with you, Janelle," Bill said. "Let's see what you can do."

Janelle slid to her knees and worked her electric guitar. She was amazing!

"Nice," Bill said. "We'll need to work on your chord changes and practice some new techniques."

Then Bill turned to me and said, "Let's hear what you've got, Mary-Kate. Give me a dominant seventh chord."

Seventh what? I forced a smile as I stretched my fingers. Then I began to play "Itsy Bitsy Spider."

"You're a joker, Mary-Kate." Bill chuckled. "Come on. Let's hear you play that chord."

My heart pounded. I had to play something. But there was only one song I remembered how to play.

I stretched my arms over my head. I cracked a few knuckles. Then I began to play . . . "Itsy Bitsy Spider."

When I was done I slowly looked up. Lark and Janelle were staring at me with wide eyes. So was Bill.

"Are you serious, Mary-Kate?" Bill said. He scratched the top of his head. "Is that all you know how to play?"

"I took my last piano lesson when I was ten," I confessed. "I quit to play softball."

"Softball?" Bill said. "Mary-Kate, you can't play 'Itsy Bitsy Spider' in a rock band!"

"I think I can play 'London Bridge,' too!" I blurted out. "Or 'Mary Had A Little Lamb.'"

Bill buried his face in his hands. He looked up and took a deep breath. "Is there any other instrument you can play, Mary-Kate?" he asked.

"Why do I have to play an instrument?" I asked. "I can sing!"

"Camp Rock 'n' Roll is all about learning new things," Bill explained. "Besides, everyone here should know how to play at least one instrument."

Except Lark, I thought.

It wasn't fair, Diary. But if I really wanted to stay at Camp Rock 'n' Roll, I had to play something!

I played the recorder in third grade, I thought. *Or was it a slide-whistle?*

Suddenly I remembered something else. . . .

Dad plays the saxophone, I thought. *He's always showing Ashley and me how to play a few tunes!*

"My dad showed me how to play the saxophone," I said quickly.

"Sax, huh?" Bill said doubtfully.

Janelle stepped forward. "I can add some electric riffs to Mary-Kate's parts," she said. "To juice it up."

Bill seemed to think about it. Then he smiled and said, "Check. I'll dig up a sax and some reeds, Mary-Kate. Then tomorrow we'll hear you play."

"Check!" I said, crossing my fingers behind my back.

Bill turned to Lark and smiled his biggest smile. "Lark, we're ready for you," he said. "But only if you're ready for us."

"Ready," Lark said.

Three roadies raced over to adjust Lark's mike. One offered her a bottle of water.

The room became so quiet, you could hear a guitar pick drop. Lark gripped the mike with both hands and sang a pretty song that had a good beat. Her voice was sweet and clear and very soft. But as I watched Lark I noticed something. She didn't sing with any spirit. She seemed sad, like she wished she didn't have to sing.

Still, when Lark finished, all the counselors cheered and clapped, as if she were some kind of rock star.

That does it! I turned to Janelle and whispered, "What's the deal? Why does everybody treat Lark like she's royalty?"

Janelle stared at me. "Don't you know?" she asked.

"Know what?" I asked.

"Lark's dad is Rodney Beecham!" Janelle whispered.

I stared at Janelle. Did I hear right? Did she just say Rodney Beecham?

"You mean the rock superstar with fifty gold records?" I squeaked. "The one who lives in a medieval castle?"

"That's the guy," Janelle said.

"Whoa!" I gasped.

Diary, no wonder Lark is treated like royalty. She's a princess, all right. A *rock* princess!

Dear Diary,

Wait until you find out how much Erin and I have in common!

"You mean you live in Chicago?" Erin squealed. "I live about half an hour outside of Chicago! I went into the city just last month for the big 4You concert."

I gave a little shriek. 4You is my favorite band. Mary-Kate's, too. "Are you a 4You fan?" I asked Erin.

"Are you kidding?" Erin said. "I know all of the guys' signs. Trent is an Aquarius. Matt is a Gemini. And David is—"

"Taurus," I cut in. "But he's on the cusp of—"

"Gemini!" Erin squealed.

All this happened last night in the rec hall. Phoebe stayed in the bunk to write letters, but Erin and I were busy finding out all about each other. Here's the best part: When we got back to the bunk, Erin gave me a 4You CD that I don't have, their live concert in Japan!

Diary, I am so lucky. Not only did I come to camp with my sister and my best friend, but I made a new friend who's practically my soul mate.

I was so psyched about being in a band with Erin and Phoebe that I couldn't wait for our first practice session. It came right after a class on reading musical notes.

Jennifer listened to each of us sing. Then she made a decision.

"You all sing great," Jennifer said. "But Erin has the strongest voice, so she should sing lead."

"Yes!" Erin cheered.

"Ashley and Phoebe, you'll both play guitar and sing backup," Jennifer said. "How's that?"

I was more excited about playing my guitar than singing. And I knew Phoebe wanted to write songs more than anything.

"I'm cool with it," I said, nodding.

"Me too," Phoebe said.

"Great!" Jennifer said with a smile. "Okay, Teen Spirit. Let's start practicing!"

While Erin practiced her keyboard, Jennifer taught Phoebe and me a technique called "hammer-ons." That's when you tap on the guitar strings while you play. Then Jennifer told us that we had to choose a song to perform.

"You can pick a song from a CD," Jennifer told us, "or write one of your own."

"Ta-daaa!" Phoebe said as she ran to her guitar case. "I wrote a song for us last night."

So that's what Phoebe was doing in the bunk last night, I realized. *She was writing a song.*

"It's called 'The Lonely Beach,'" Phoebe said, holding up a sheet of paper.

"'The Lonely Beach,'" Erin said thoughtfully. Her eyes lit up. "Is it about a beach party that gets rained out?"

Phoebe shook her head. "It's about saving our beaches by protecting the environment," she explained.

Erin blinked her long blond eyelashes. "That is so intense!" she said. "But when I think beach, I think clambakes, beach volleyball, and cute suntanned guys."

"Excuse me," Phoebe said, "but serious singers do not sing about clambakes."

"And rock stars don't sing about rotting driftwood!" Erin shot back. She wrinkled her nose. "Ewwww!"

Phoebe looked straight at me. "Ashley?" she whispered. "What do you think?"

Me? I was thinking about all those clambakes, beach volleyball games, and cute suntanned hotties—

Jennifer's voice interrupted my thoughts. "Why don't we try singing Phoebe's song?" she asked. "All bands should be open to new ideas."

Erin blew her long blond bangs away from her forehead. "Okay," she said. "Whatever."

Jennifer ducked out of the room for a minute and came back with three copies of "The Lonely Beach." After studying the lyrics, we spent the next hour coming up with a tune.

"Let's try it!" Jennifer told us.

Erin played a few chords. Then she began to sing. . . .

"'I know a beach somewhere—hey, baby, baby— a beach where nobody cares—hey, baby, baby—'"

"Stop!" Phoebe exclaimed. She raised an eyebrow at Erin. "'Hey, baby, baby'? That's not in my song!"

"Bands should be open to new ideas," Erin said with a little grin. "Right?"

"I guess," Phoebe said, but she didn't sound happy about it.

It was obvious that Phoebe and Erin were on different pages. *They'll work it out*, I told myself. And I had to admit—I liked the "hey, baby, baby's."

It took a few tries, but we played Phoebe's song from beginning to end. I couldn't believe how good we sounded. Before we knew it, our first practice session was over.

"Great job, Teen Spirit!" Jennifer said. "We'll meet tomorrow, same time, same place."

Erin stayed behind to pack up her keyboard. Phoebe and I left the music building together.

"Aren't you totally psyched that we're playing your song, Phoebe?" I asked.

"*My* song?" Phoebe cried. "Erin just turned my endangered beach into spring break!"

"She just tweaked it a little," I said.

"*Ruined* is more like it," Phoebe muttered. "And the name 'Teen Spirit' sounds like some dippy perfume."

I stopped walking and stared at Phoebe. "If you didn't like the name, why didn't you say so?" I asked.

"Because you spoke for both of us!" Phoebe said.

I stared at Phoebe as she walked away. I *had* spoken for us both. But I'd honestly thought Phoebe liked the name.

I wish I could make Phoebe feel better about our band, I thought. *But how?*

I heard giggling and looked up. A country-rock band called The Corral Chicks was coming out of a small cabin. The girls were all wearing Western-style costumes.

"Yee-haaa!" one of them shouted.

They strutted away and I peeked inside. Shelves and racks were filled with all kinds of costumes and outrageous hats. A counselor was draping a black velvet cape on a plastic hanger. She looked up at me and smiled.

"This is the wardrobe cabin," she said. "Do you need costumes for your band?"

"Not yet, thanks," I answered.

I couldn't stop staring at the costumes.

Wow! I thought. *This is just like the drama department's costume room back at White Oak. The one Phoebe and I work in for all the plays.*

That's when I had the most amazing idea. . . .

Every band has a stylist. And Phoebe is great at costume design, I thought. *She'd have tons of fun planning Teen Spirit's look!*

And if Phoebe's happier, the whole band will be happier. Diary, why didn't I think of this before?

Chapter 5

Wednesday

Dear Diary,

This morning after breakfast, Bunk
Elvis went straight to arts and crafts.
Even the art projects here are all about

rock. Some of us silk-screened tees with the logos of
classic rock groups like The Who and Blue Oyster
Cult. Others jazzed up their own clothes with
sequins and studs.

I added some studs to a fake leather bracelet.
Lark sat next to me, wrapping red ribbons around
her tambourine.

"Do you really live in a castle, Lark?" I asked.

Lark didn't even look up. "In other words," she
said, "you want to know all about my dad."

"Not really," I said. "I want to know about *you*."

"That's a switch," Lark said. "Most kids want to
be friends with me because my dad is Rodney
Beecham. Then they lose interest when I tell them I
hardly ever see my dad."

"You don't?" I asked. "How come?"

"My mom and dad are divorced," Lark said.
"I've lived with my mom in New Mexico since I
was three. The only time my dad shows up is when
he's doing a concert in Santa Fe."

"I didn't know that," I said. "But I want to be

good friends with you no matter who your dad is."

Lark gave me a smirk. "Yeah, right."

"It's true!" I insisted. "We're in the same band, right? So we have to be tight!"

Lark sighed. "I'm sorry you got bumped from singing, Mary-Kate," she said. "It's because of my dad."

"What do you mean?"

"A cable station is taping a Rodney Beecham special," she explained. "Dad's publicity guy came up with the idea of us singing together in the show. So Dad let Stella know he wanted me to practice singing lead. He said he might even perform with our band in the Battle of the Bands."

"Wow!" I exclaimed. "How cool is that?"

"Not for me," Lark admitted. "It's not as if Dad thought of the idea himself. It's, like, he's only interested in me when it helps his career. If my dad knew me better, he'd know that I don't even like singing in public. He doesn't even know what I like to do."

No wonder Lark doesn't look happy when she sings, I thought.

"Here," I said, giving Lark my leather bracelet. "Consider this a friendship bracelet. And it has nothing to do with your dad!"

Lark slipped the bracelet on and smiled. "Thanks, Mary-Kate," she said. "Maybe it'll bring me luck."

"What kind of luck?" I asked.

"Even though I don't want to sing on TV, I still want to do a good job," Lark admitted. "Maybe then my dad will want to spend more time with me."

"You'll be great, Lark," I said. "You have a beautiful voice. Just keep singing the way you always do."

I could use some of my own luck, Diary. The first round—the harmony round—is this weekend, and I have to show Bill that I can play the saxophone!

Dear Diary,

Right after lunch I called a Teen Spirit meeting down at the lake. The three of us sat beneath a big leafy tree.

"Why are we here?" Erin asked. She nodded at Phoebe's guitar and giggled. "To sing 'Kumbaya'?"

"I happen to like 'Kumbaya,'" Phoebe said.

"Listen up, Teen Spirit," I said. "It's time we talked about what our band's going to wear."

"You mean costumes?" Phoebe asked.

My plan was already working. Phoebe's face was lighting up like the Fourth of July!

"Costumes are *exactly* what I mean," I said. "Music isn't just about music anymore—it's about image."

"What if we wear all black?" Phoebe suggested. "Maybe black velvet with lots of silver jewelry."

"Sounds good," I agreed.

"Sure." Erin groaned. "If you're playing classical music."

Phoebe frowned. "What do you mean by that?"

Erin stood up. "Black and silver just sounds a little . . . formal. And serious. When I think of Teen Spirit, I think fresh eye-popping color. I think . . . pink!"

"Pink?" Phoebe repeated.

"I think everything we wear should be pink," Erin explained. "Pink tees, pink pants, flip-flops—"

I smiled as I pictured the band all pinked-out. Pink is one of my favorite colors.

"Even better, let's forget the name 'Teen Spirit,'" Erin went on. "We need something edgier. Something that tells the whole world who we are. Something like, Electric Pink."

"We could wear pink makeup, too," I said, jumping up. "Pink blush, lipstick, eye shadow—"

"We could even give ourselves pink pedicures!" Erin said. "And I think you should go electric, Ashley."

"You mean play an electric guitar?" I asked.

Erin nodded. "It goes with our image."

I liked the idea of me all in pink playing electric guitar. I held up my hand to high-five Erin.

"What do you think, Phoebe?" I asked.

Phoebe stared at me long and hard. She finally blinked and said, "You've *got* to be kidding."

"Here we go." Erin sighed.

"We're a band—not cartoon characters!" Phoebe said. "I didn't even bring pink clothes. The only pink outfit I own is a coat from the nineteen fifties. And that's back home in San Francisco!"

"I'm sorry you don't like my idea, Phoebe," Erin said. "But Ashley does. I guess you're outnumbered."

Phoebe shot me a look. "Ashley?" she said.

My stomach flip-flopped. I was in the middle again!

"Um . . ." I said. "Maybe we can wear Phoebe's silver jewelry with the outfits?" I smiled at Phoebe.

"As long as the jewelry has pink beads," Erin said.

Phoebe groaned. She picked up her guitar and walked away. I could almost see steam coming out of her ears.

"What planet is she from, anyway?" Erin asked.

"She's just—" I started.

"Never mind. It's not important," Erin said. Then she walked down to the lake to skim stones.

That was mean, I thought. But what could I do? Phoebe and Erin were so different. They might never agree on anything. And as for me . . .

Diary, can I help it if I like Erin's ideas more than Phoebe's? But now I feel totally trapped between my old friend and my new friend. Why does it have to be this way, Diary? Why can't we all just get along?

Chapter 6

Thursday

Dear Diary,

As of today, the group formerly known as The Diva Dollz is Xtreme! The name change was Janelle's idea.
She said whenever she heard "Diva Dollz," she thought of a bunch of big-eyed dolls with stringy hair and giant feet.

And, as of last night, I started practicing on a borrowed sax. Well, sort of. I've mostly been trying to remember where my fingers should go.

"What do you think?" I asked Ashley after practicing in the bunk. "Do I sound like Kenny G?"

"More like Lisa Simpson!" Ashley said with a giggle. "But not bad, Mary-Kate. Not bad!"

This morning after breakfast I ran back to the bunk to practice more. Janelle came, too. She wanted to look for her lucky guitar pick.

"Eww," Janelle said as I played.

I looked up. "Am I that bad?"

"It's not your playing," Janelle said. "I was just thinking of all the campers who must have spit into that thing by now."

"Gross. I never thought of that," I said. "I'd better wash the mouthpiece in soap and water."

"No good." Janelle shook her head. "Brass

instruments need to be cleaned with a special kind of polish."

Janelle ran out of the bunk and was back a few minutes later with a jar of polish. "I borrowed this from Stella," she said. "Rub it all over the sax until it shines."

I opened the jar and dipped a paper towel into it. Then I rubbed the mouthpiece good.

"It's a saxophone, not a magic lamp," Janelle said, giggling. "Come on or we'll be late for practice."

I quickly packed the sax into its case. Then Janelle and I raced to the music building. Bill and Lark were already inside.

"Before we talk about your first song, I want to hear Mary-Kate play the sax," Bill said.

"Right," I said. I slipped in a new reed. I held the sax with both hands and rested it on my right hip. I put the mouthpiece between my lips and blew a note. Suddenly the grossest taste exploded through my whole mouth!

I felt my whole face scrunching up like a raisin. I tried to keep playing, but the sour taste was too horrible!

"Are you okay, Mary-Kate?" Bill asked.

"Pleeegh!" I cried, pulling the sax away. I stuck my tongue out and sputtered, "Phew, phew, phhh-hhew! Yuck!"

"Uh-oh," Janelle said. "I think you were supposed to wipe the polish off, Mary-Kate."

"Now you tell me," I said, still sputtering.

Everyone waited while I scrubbed the waxy polish off the mouthpiece. Then Bill said, "Shall we try again?"

I gripped the sax and began to play. The sour taste was gone. But not the sour notes.

"Didn't you say you took sax lessons?" Bill asked.

"It's been a while," I confessed. "And now every time I play a note, I think about that nasty taste!"

Bill ran his hand through his hair. "Do the best you can." He sighed. "I think you'll get the hang of it soon."

Bill gave me a lesson and showed me where all the notes were. I played the sax for the rest of the practice session, but I couldn't stop tasting that gross taste. By the time practice was over, I hated playing the saxophone!

I decided I *had* to find another instrument to play in the band. But I wasn't going to tell Bill until I found it.

"Ashley," I said later, "I need your help."

Ashley was alone in the bunk. She was sitting on her bed and practicing chords on a brand-new electric guitar.

41

"Watch what Jennifer taught me," Ashley said. "It's called bending."

Ashley bent the guitar strings as she played. It made a really neat wailing sound.

Her acoustic guitar was leaning against the bed. I picked it up and said, "Remember when I used to play this?"

"Yeah, you were pretty good," Ashley said.

"You just gave me the most awesome idea!" I said. I sat down beside her. "If you'll give me some brushup lessons, I can play the guitar in my band."

"What?" Ashley squeaked. "Mary-Kate, learning to play an instrument takes lots of practice."

"It will all come back to me when I start to play," I explained. "I just need to go over the basics so I can fake it while I sing backup. Please, Ashley? Pleeeeeeease?"

"Okay," Ashley finally said. "But just the basics."

Ashley was a great teacher. She showed me how to play minor and major chords. Most of it *did* come back as I practiced. I thought I sounded pretty good, too.

"You're the best, Ashley." I imitated Rodney Beecham, raising my fist. "Now I'm all ready to roooock!"

I left Bunk Elvis and found Bill coming out of the music building. He looked surprised to see the guitar. "Why didn't you tell me you play guitar, Mary-Kate?"

"You didn't ask," I said with a grin.

Diary, I've been practicing ever since, and I already have something to show for it. Perfect chord changes—and a honking blister on the middle of my thumb. Ouch!

Diary, today was the absolute worst!

It was the first day Phoebe, Erin, and I showed up at band practice as Electric Pink. Erin wore a pink miniskirt, pink tank, pink flip-flops, and the pinkest lip gloss I've ever seen. I wore pink painter's pants, a rose-colored tube top, and my pink ballet flats.

The only one not pinked-out was Phoebe. She showed up in a red-and-white-checked blouse and red shorts.

"We were supposed to wear pink," Erin said.

Phoebe folded her arms over her chest. "I told you I didn't bring any pink clothes," she said.

"But red and white makes pink!" I put in quickly.

Phoebe and Erin stopped arguing once we began jamming. The Lonely Beach song sounded great.

After practice we headed back to Bunk Elvis to drop off our instruments. Our other bunk mates weren't there, but our laundry bags were. The camp sends out our dirty laundry every Wednesday and returns it clean the next day.

Phoebe opened her laundry bag and gasped. She started yanking out her clothes. "My light-colored clothing!" she wailed. "It all came back pink!"

We dumped Phoebe's clothes on her bed. Sure enough, they were all different shades of pink.

"Here's the culprit," I said, picking up one bright red sock. "Red stuff washed in hot water usually runs."

"I didn't put that sock in there!" Phoebe said, staring at the sock. "I don't even have red socks!"

"Look on the bright side," Erin said and giggled. "Now you'll have plenty of pink clothes for the band!"

Phoebe whirled around and pointed at Erin. "You did this, didn't you?" she demanded. "Because I didn't have any pink clothes. It was your idea of a joke!"

Erin stared at Phoebe with her big blue eyes. Then she stuck her chin out and said, "I did nothing of the kind!"

"Then who did?" Phoebe demanded.

Erin started out of the bunk. "I'm out of here," she called over her shoulder. "See you later, *Ashley*."

"Why didn't you say something?" Phoebe asked me. "It's obvious Erin put that red sock in my wash."

"She said she *didn't*, Phoebe," I reminded her.

"And you believe her?" Phoebe asked.

"Yes, I do," I said. "Why don't you just let it go?"

"Let it go?" Phoebe cried. "There you go again, taking Erin's side. Just because you think she's so cool!"

Diary, I couldn't believe what was happening. I've seen Phoebe mad before—but never at me.

"I'm not taking sides, Phoebe!" I protested.

"Yeah, right." Phoebe turned away and started sorting her pink laundry.

The truth is, Diary, I really did believe Erin.

It's only the first week of camp, I told myself. *Phoebe and Erin will calm down, and things will get better.*

Chapter 7

Friday

Dear Diary,

The first round of the Battle of the Bands is tomorrow, and I think I'm ready. At practice this morning I knew all the notes across the fret board and parts of our song, too.

Janelle lent me her lucky guitar pick. She'd caught it at a Gag Reflex concert, which is why it's lucky.

This morning we picked out our outfits for the first performance. Janelle chose baggy camouflage pants and a tuxedo jacket. I picked out a studded jean miniskirt and a black velvet blazer. Lark says she's going to wear her own jeans and a plain gray tank top.

"I don't want to stand out," Lark explained.

After lunch I sat on the back step of our bunk and stared out at the rolling green hills. That's when I saw it—a lone soccer ball lying on the field.

If there's just one problem about Camp Rock 'n' Roll so far, it's this: I'm going through serious sports withdrawal! Most kids here would rather play their instruments than a good game of softball.

I know this is a music camp, I thought. *But even*

Madonna played softball once. So what if it was in a movie?

I jogged over to the ball and dribbled it across the grass. I pulled my right foot all the way back to shoot it across the field. Just as I was about to kick, another foot appeared out of nowhere to hook the ball.

My jaw dropped open when I saw it was Lark's.

"Your goal is that tree behind you," she said with a grin. "Mine is the boulder across the field."

"First one to score three goals takes the match," I said, grinning back.

In no time Lark and I were into our game. I thought my soccer skills were pretty good, but they were no match for Lark's. She had the best fakes and speed dribbling I've ever seen. She shot the ball like a pro, and her footwork was totally awesome!

"Where did you learn to play like that?" I asked when, about ten minutes later, Lark scored her third goal.

"I've always loved soccer," Lark said. "Ever since I was a little kid."

As we set up for another match, Lark told me about her soccer team at home. "Most of the time I'm the goalie, but what I really like is playing forward," Lark explained. Her whole face glowed as she talked about soccer. For the first time since camp started, Lark looked happy. *Really* happy!

"I didn't think rock princesses were into sports," I joked. "I thought they spent all their time backstage at concerts, fashion shows, music awards—"

"Not this rock princess," Lark cut in. "My life with my mom is just like everybody else's. Which is why I want to be treated like everybody else."

"You are," I said. "I'll bet half the kids here don't even know you're Rodney Beecham's daughter."

"Lark, I've been looking for you!" Another girl was running toward us. It was Katie Lund, from Bunk Tina Turner.

"Maybe Katie wants to play, too," I said.

Katie stopped in front of Lark. She held out a pen. "Can you please sign my sneaker?" Katie asked.

"You want me to sign your sneaker?" Lark said. "Why?"

"Du-uh!" Katie giggled. "Because you're Rodney Beecham's daughter, that's why!"

Lark shot me an I-told-you-so look.

She looked totally miserable as she signed Katie's sneaker. It's clear she's not happy at Camp Rock 'n' Roll.

Maybe Lark would have been happier in another camp, Diary. *Soccer* camp!

Camp Rock 'n' Roll

Dear Diary,

Today in practice, Phoebe, Erin, and I ran through our song three times.

"Way to go!" Jennifer cheered after our third run-through. "You guys are in perfect harmony."

If only we were in perfect harmony all the time, I thought a little sadly.

Jennifer wished us luck on the first round. Then she left for an instructors meeting.

"We should keep on practicing for tomorrow," I said.

"Good idea," Phoebe agreed.

"I have a better idea," Erin said, smiling slyly. "Let's spy on the other bands."

"Spy? That is so immature," Phoebe said.

I had a bad feeling that another feud was coming on soon.

"I'm sure Erin doesn't mean *spy*," I said quickly. "She probably means we should get an idea of what we'll be up against tomorrow. Right, Erin?"

"Right," Erin said. "It'll be superfun!"

"Come on, Phoebe," I said.

The three of us left our instruments in the music building. We walked across the campgrounds. I heard music coming from one of the bunks. We followed the sound to Bunk Elton John and peeked through a window. The girls from a group called Stringz were practicing. They were playing a cello, a fiddle, and an electric violin. Their song sounded like a rock 'n' roll version of something I'd heard before.

"That song is called 'Greensleeves,'" Phoebe whispered. "They say King Henry VIII wrote it for his true love, Anne Boleyn."

"Before or after he chopped off her head?" Erin whispered.

"You mean you actually know history?" Phoebe asked Erin. "I'm impressed."

I watched Stringz play. The song was hundreds of years old, but they made it sound totally hot. I never knew string instruments could rock like that.

Erin giggled. "Wouldn't it be funny if somebody greased their bows before the first round? So that when they started playing—zing—the bows would fly out of their hands!"

"Ha!" I laughed. Then I clapped my hand over my mouth.

Stringz stopped playing. We ducked just before they looked in our direction.

"Is somebody there?" one girl called.

Still ducking, the three of us scurried away. Erin and I were giggling. Phoebe was not.

"I can't believe what you said, Erin," Phoebe said. "About greasing their bows."

"I was just kidding!" Erin exclaimed.

"Really?" Phoebe asked. "Just like when you put the red sock into my—"

"You guys!" I had to stop them before they started arguing. "What do you want to do next—practice? Hang out?"

"Practice," Phoebe said.

"Practice can wait," Erin said. "We still have to check out The Corral Chicks. And Venus. And Fresh Start."

"No way!" Phoebe said. "We need to practice."

This time I was *not* going to be in the middle.

"Do what you want," I said. "*I'm* going back to the bunk to write a letter to my dad."

I felt Erin and Phoebe watch me as I headed toward Bunk Elvis. It was the first time I hadn't taken sides. Would they both be mad at *me* now?

Mary-Kate was in the bunk when I walked in. She was sitting on the floor, playing her guitar.

"Ashley, check it out," Mary-Kate said. "I can play Dad's favorite song, 'Stairway to Heaven.'"

I sat on the floor and hugged my knees to my chest. "At least someone is having a good time," I said.

I told Mary-Kate about Phoebe and Erin. "I want

to be friends with both Phoebe *and* Erin," I explained. "But I'm always in the middle of their arguments."

Mary-Kate raised an eyebrow. "Didn't you promise Phoebe you'd stick with her all through camp?" she asked.

"Yeah," I said slowly.

Mary-Kate gave me a little smile. "So?" She looked down at her guitar and continued playing.

I kind of knew what Mary-Kate was saying. I *did* promise to stick by Phoebe, no matter what. But why did that seem to mean I couldn't be friends with Erin?

Chapter 8

Saturday

Dear Diary,

Last night I had a dream about the first round of the Battle of the Bands but woke up before I could find out who won. Bummer. Especially since today is the day.

Everyone was totally stoked at breakfast. Then we all ran back to our bunks to change into our costumes.

I was good to go in my velvet jacket and studded skirt. Janelle had on her baggy pants and tux jacket. And the streaks in her hair were bright blue!

"It's called Blueberry Blaze," Janelle said. "Don't you guys want to jazz up your hair with a little color?"

"Um . . . I'll pass," I said with a smile.

"I just want the rounds to be *over*," Lark said.

The three of us walked to the camp theater. As soon as we got inside, I saw the judges. Clarence and Sophie were chatting. Terrence was busy studying some papers.

"He doesn't look happy," I whispered to Janelle.

"Does he *ever*?" Janelle whispered back.

We sat down on the hard wooden theater seats. I

saw Ashley and waved. She waved back and mouthed, "Good luck!"

The roadies were onstage setting up drums and a keyboard. On the floor were cables for the mikes and amps.

Stella Vickers walked up to the center microphone. "Let's kick off the harmony round with Fresh Start," she said. "Show us what you got, girls!"

Fresh Start climbed onstage. They were all wearing low-rise pants and patterned tops. One girl had a trumpet. After a sound-check, they began to play.

The trumpet-girl took turns playing and rapping. Another girl played keyboards, and a third played drums. She banged the drums so fast, her hands were a blur!

"Give it up for Fresh Start!" Stella cheered. "Now let's see what our judges thought. Clarence?"

"Ain't it funky now?" Clarence exclaimed. "The drums were a little heavy, but the rest was cool. Way cool."

"For me, too," Sophie said. "As the first band, you were under a lot of pressure, but you handled yourself like real pros. Bravo!"

The judges were being fair. At least that's what I thought before we got to Terrence. . . .

"Fresh Start?" Terrence said mockingly. "For a

band called Fresh Start, you sounded a bit stale to me."

Fresh Start's smiles vanished.

"You need to slow down a bit, too," Terrence said. "At times that trumpet sounded like a machine gun!"

Fresh Start sulked off the stage. They scored a six out of a possible ten. Not bad. Not great either.

"Did you bring my lucky guitar pick?" Janelle asked.

"Yeah, why?" I said.

"We're going to need all the luck we can get!"

Next up were The Corral Chicks in their denim Western gear. Two of them played guitar, and one played rhythm on an old-fashioned metal washboard.

"Had I known you had a washboard, I would have brought my dirty socks," Terrence told them. "And I could tell you were nervous," he went on, "just by the way you played."

The Corral Chicks scored five out of ten.

I saw Lark from the corner of my eye. Talk about nervous! She was trembling so hard, her tambourine shook.

"Next band up is Xtreme!" Stella announced.

That's us! I thought, my heart pounding.

Bill gave us a thumbs-up sign, and we hurried

up onto the stage. One roadie helped Janelle plug her guitar into an amp, but about five roadies helped adjust Lark's mike.

I gazed into the audience and saw Ashley. She was giving me two thumbs-ups. I looked at Terrence. He was sipping a cup of coffee with a bored look on his face.

The roadies ran off the stage and the audience became quiet. Janelle played the first few chords. Lark began to sing in a shaky voice. That was my cue to start strumming.

Come on, lucky pick, I thought. *Don't let me down!*

After a few riffs I felt the music start to take over. I forgot about everything except playing and how good that felt. Just as I was totally rocking out, the guitar pick bounced off the strings and flew out of my hand. I froze as the pick made a splash landing in Terrence's coffee cup!

Lark stared at me with wide eyes.

"So much for lucky picks," Janelle mumbled.

Terrence fished out the wet pick. "I take my coffee with sugar and a little cream," he said. "Not guitar picks."

"S-s-sorry," I stammered.

Stella smiled at me and said, "Start again, Xtreme. And try fingerpicking this time, Mary-Kate."

We started from the top. I began to relax as I

plucked the melody with my fingers. When I glanced at Janelle, her knees were bent and her head was bobbing back and forth.

I've got to pump it up, too, I thought.

I remembered the bending technique Ashley showed me. I wondered if it would work on an acoustic guitar. I bent the string and—POP—it broke!

Oh, noooo! I thought.

I held up my busted guitar. The broken string waved back and forth like undercooked spaghetti on a fork!

Janelle stopped playing. Lark stopped singing.

"What we have here is an Xtreme disaster," Terrence said. "*Two* extreme disasters in a row."

"Broken strings can happen to any guitarist, Mary-Kate," Stella called out. "Do you want to go on?"

"W-w-with what?" I stammered.

One of the roadies ran over to me. He handed me an acoustic guitar. Xtreme started again. This time we got through the whole song without a hitch.

"You got off to a rocky start but proved you can come back," Sophie said. "Well done, Xtreme."

"Way to go," Clarence agreed.

I looked at Terrence. He shrugged with one shoulder and finally said, "Lark was a bit nervous.

Janelle's guitar sounds like it needs a little tuning. Mary-Kate really needs to work on playing the right notes, but the song turned out pretty good."

I breathed a big sigh of relief. Especially when we got a seven out of ten!

Backstage, Janelle hugged me. "We did it!"

"Xtreme rules!" I cheered.

I was so happy, I almost forgot that I'd had two guitar disasters in a row. But then I remembered the flying pick and the broken string. Diary, I think something is telling me that I should *not* be playing guitar!

Dear Diary,

Poor Mary-Kate. A busted string can happen to the biggest rock stars, but her heart just isn't in the guitar, or the sax, or the keyboard. She wants to sing!

Stringz was the next band up after Xtreme. Their version of "Greensleeves" got them a score of six.

Then it was time for Electric Pink!

I was so psyched when we climbed onto the stage. Erin plugged in her keyboard. Phoebe and I practiced a few chords. Phoebe was wearing a pale pink halter and capris, both of which used to be white—before the red sock got to them.

Phoebe mouthed, "Good luck."

I mouthed, "You too." I was pretty relieved that things seemed okay between us now.

"Electric Pink, do your stuff!" Stella announced.

We began to play "The Lonely Beach," and something awesome slowly happened: Everything seemed to gel. Erin's voice was stronger than ever. Phoebe and I jumped in with the chorus at just the right times.

As I played my guitar, I took a quick glance at the judges. Clarence and Sophie were swaying in their seats. Even Terrence was tapping his pencil against his cup.

"'What goes out always comes in with the tide,'" Erin sang. "'So, hey, baby, baby, don't run and hide!'"

When the song was over, we took our bows. The sound of everyone cheering gave me major goose bumps—the good kind!

"You're definitely high voltage, Electric Pink!" Clarence said. "Right on, girls, right on!"

"You proved to everyone that you're really in the pink," Sophie said. "And that's something to be proud of."

I gulped. What would Terrence have to say?

"I'm not going to lie," Terrence said. "You left the last stanza behind like some beached whale. . . . But not bad, Electric Pink . . . not bad at all."

Stella added up the judges' scores. "Electric Pink's in the lead with an eight!"

Backstage, we all jumped up and down. "Electric Pink is number one!" I cheered. "We even made Terrence smile!"

"Was my pink plan totally brilliant or what?" Erin asked. "It really helped our score!"

"So did my song," Phoebe pointed out.

"As soon as I added the 'hey, baby, baby's,'" Erin said. She picked up her keyboard and headed back to the seats.

"Did you hear what she said, Ashley?" Phoebe asked.

"I heard," I said. "But instead of fighting, the three of us should be celebrating a great score!"

"The *three* of us," Phoebe said. "Why does it always have to be the three of us? Why can't the *two* of us have fun together like we do in school?"

Phoebe had a point. We always did fun things together back in school. So why not in camp?

"Why don't we go kayaking on the lake?" I asked.

Phoebe smiled. "You mean the two of us?" she asked.

"Just you and me," I promised.

Chapter 9

Sunday

Dear Diary,

Atomic Pizza! That's our band's new name, as of last night. Janelle came up with it while we were eating pizza muffins for dinner.

Today we found out that the next round—the vocals round—is on Tuesday. Janelle and I will sing backup. Lark is still the lead vocalist.

After practice, the three of us stayed in the music room to talk about the next round. I stared down at my guitar. Bill fixed the broken string last night, but I didn't feel like playing it anymore. If only I could be as into an instrument as the rest of the kids were.

"Okay, Atomic Pizza," Janelle said. "What song should we sing in the next round?"

"How about the same song we sang in the last round?" Lark asked.

"Why don't we come up with something new?" I asked.

The three of us sat cross-legged on the floor and started brainstorming. It took us two hours, but we came up with lyrics to a song we called "Just Like You."

Lark tried singing it, but it didn't sound right. She couldn't get the beat.

"It's like this." I jumped up and pulled a pair of drumsticks off a shelf. I looked around for drums, but there weren't any in the room. So I picked up an aluminum wastebasket from the corner and tipped it over. Using the drumsticks, I began tapping out the beat.

"What do you think, Lark?" I asked. "Do you hear the rhythm now?"

Lark and Janelle were staring at me

"That is so metal, Mary-Kate," Janelle said.

"What is?" I asked, still tapping on the can. I was really getting into it.

"The way you're drumming," Janelle explained, "the sound totally rocks!"

"My mom once took me to a show called *Pulse*," Lark said. "The drummers were drumming on basins, buckets, cans—anything that made a noise. You sound just like them."

Basins? Buckets? Cans? Suddenly I had the best idea!

"Meet me outside our bunk," I said, slipping the drumsticks into my back pocket. "In about half an hour."

"Where are you going?" Janelle asked.

"No time to explain," I said as I raced out the door.

I ran all over camp collecting anything that I could make a beat on—buckets, basins, even an empty jumbo-size can of baked beans from the mess hall. I set them up in front of our bunk. Then I sat down on an upside-down bucket and found the rhythm.

Janelle and Lark hurried over.

"Go, Mary-Kate!" Lark cheered.

Soon, a group of instructors and campers came over to see what was going on. I didn't stop playing. I was having the best time trying out different sounds and beats.

"Play it, girl!" Ivy shouted.

For my big finish, I twirled the drumsticks between my fingers, then tossed them in the air. Everyone went wild, even though I only caught one drumstick. (I'll have to work on that, Diary.)

I saw Bill standing nearby.

"Hey, Bill. Can I drum on these buckets and basins for the next round?" I asked. "I promise I'll wash out the crusty cans so they don't smell like baked beans."

Bill shook his head. "Buckets, basins, and cans aren't exactly musical instruments, Mary-Kate," he said.

My heart sank. I'd finally found an instrument that fit me, and he wouldn't let me play it!

Stella stepped through the crowd and smiled. "Oh, Bill, lighten up!" she said. "Music is music, no matter how it's played."

Stella looked at me and said, "Try it out, Mary-Kate. And have fun with it."

"Ye-es!" I cheered. I took hold of both drumsticks and began to practice.

Diary, I know I'll never be a famous rock star playing buckets and basins. But, you know what? I'm having too much fun to care!

Dear Diary,

This morning on our break, Phoebe and I changed into swimsuits and went down to the lake. Buddy-time at last! Erin wasn't around, so I didn't feel bad about not including her. But when Phoebe and I reached the lake, all the kayaks and canoes were out on the water.

"Great," I said. "I really wanted to go kayaking. What do we do now?"

Phoebe kicked off her flip-flops. "Race you to the lake!" she called.

Phoebe and I charged into the water. We had tons of fun swimming and splashing each other. It was just like at school when we'd pal around for hours—just the two of us.

We swam back to shore and sat on our towels. I hugged my knees and gazed out at the lake. Phoebe lay on her back and stared up at the clouds. I could hear her singing something softly to herself. It sounded nice.

"What's that you're singing?" I asked.

"Just a song I've been making up in my head," Phoebe said. "You'll think it's corny."

"Try me," I urged.

"It's about the world coming together," Phoebe said. "But it's not finished yet."

"Then let's finish it," I said. "Maybe Electric Pink can sing it in the next round."

Phoebe grabbed her beach bag. She pulled out a pen and some stationery. Then we got to work writing lyrics.

In about an hour we wrote a whole song called "When the World Comes Together."

"Phoebe, I love it!" I exclaimed.

"Even though it has a message?" Phoebe said.

"It's a great message," I said. "What kid wouldn't want the world to come together?"

"What about Erin?" Phoebe asked. "What if she doesn't want to sing it?"

"We'll sing it, anyway," I declared.

We stood up and high-fived.

"Why didn't we think of this before?" I asked.

"You mean writing a song together?" Phoebe asked.

"Spending more time together!" I said.

Phoebe and I were about to roll up our towels when—

"Yo! Dudettes!"

We spun around. Erin was on the lake, waving from a bright red kayak. "Who wants to go kayaking?" she called.

"Are you finished with the kayak, Erin?" I asked.

"No," Erin called. "But I could sure use some company. Hop in, Ashley!"

I looked at the kayak Erin was using. It was a double kayak, designed for two people. With Erin inside, there was room for only one more.

"No, thanks," I called over the water. "There's not enough room for the three of us."

"Come on, Ashley. Just for a short ride," Erin called.

"Well . . ." I turned to Phoebe. "Would it be okay?"

"Go for it," Phoebe told me.

"Really?" I asked.

"You wanted to go kayaking," Phoebe said. "I guess I can find something else to do."

I looked at Phoebe, then at Erin. Phoebe didn't seem to mind, so . . .

"Ready or not, here I come!" I shouted.

The water splashed as I ran into the lake. Erin paddled the kayak into the shallow part, and I climbed in.

We paddled in perfect sync for a few minutes. Then Erin splashed me with her paddle and I splashed her back. Soon we were both splashing each other and laughing hysterically. I turned my head and saw Phoebe. She was still standing on the bank and she was frowning.

Is Phoebe angry? I wondered. *She can't be, can she?*

Erin and I had fun kayaking, but I couldn't stop wondering why Phoebe seemed so mad. Later I found her alone in our bunk, writing postcards.

"Phoebe, are you okay?" I asked.

"Do you care?" Phoebe said. She glared at me through her blue-frame glasses.

"Of course I care," I said. "What's going on?"

"I can't believe you did that, Ashley!"

"Did what?" I asked.

"You went kayaking with Erin," Phoebe said. "If you'd really wanted to hang with me, you would have told her no!"

Did I have water in my ears? Was I hearing right? Was Phoebe mad at me for doing something she had told me to do?

"Phoebe, you said it was okay for me to go kayaking," I reminded her. "You said you'd do something else."

"I only said that because I wanted to see what you would do," Phoebe said.

"What?" I cried. "You mean it was—a test?"

Phoebe didn't answer.

I heard some loud banging behind the bunk. Through the back window I saw Mary-Kate drumming on a bunch of cans. *Is there a full moon or something?* I wondered.

"Meet my new set of drums!" Mary-Kate said as I went outside. "Stella said I can play them in the next round!"

"And after the round you can recycle them," I joked. But I didn't feel much like laughing.

I sat down on the grass next to Mary-Kate and told her the latest. "Why is Phoebe being so unfair?" I asked.

"I guess it's hard to be fair when you think your best friend is slipping away," Mary-Kate said.

"But I'm not." I shook my head. "I don't get it."

"Think about it," Mary-Kate said. "Phoebe doesn't like you spending so much time with Erin."

"So what am I supposed to do?" I asked. "Choose only one friend?"

"No," Mary-Kate said. "You have to find some way for Erin and Phoebe to be friends so you can *all* be friends!"

"I know." I sighed. "But it's not that easy!"

Any bright ideas, Diary?

Chapter 10

Monday

Dear Diary,

Crush! That's our band's new
name, starting today. Janelle came up
with that one when she confessed she
has a crush on a roadie named Hank. And guess
what else happened today? Just as Crush was about
to practice, Stella walked into our music room with
a huge surprise. . . .

"You got another care package, Lark," Stella said.
She smiled so wide, I could see her gums. "It's from
your dad!"

Lark's mouth tightened into a thin line. "Oh . . .
terrific," she said.

The package was from London again. It was
smaller than the last one. I was dying to know what
was inside. "Aren't you going to open it, Lark?"
Stella asked.

"Yeah, aren't you curious?" Bill added.

Lark shrugged. "I'll open it when I get back to
my bunk," she replied. "It's probably no big deal."

"Hey, *anything* from Rodney Beecham is a big
deal!" Bill exclaimed. "He's the big cheese of rock!"

"Open it now!" Stella pleaded. "Go ahead!"

Lark sucked in her breath as she tore open the package. "It's sheet music," she said. "And a tape."

There was a note inside too. Lark's face dropped as she read it. "Um . . . my dad wrote a song for our band," she told us. "He wants us to sing it in the next round."

"Yes!" Bill cheered. "My band is going to sing a Rodney Beecham original! How cool is that?"

Janelle and I exchanged grins. We were pretty stoked about singing a Rodney Beecham song, too.

"Sorry," Lark said, quietly packing everything back into the box. "I'm not doing it."

"Why not?" Stella and Bill asked at the same time.

"The song was probably his manager's idea," Lark said. "Just like sending me to this camp. My dad is probably going along with it because it'll make him look good."

The room got quiet. The Corral Chicks and some girls from Stringz were standing at the door, listening in.

Stella put her arm around Lark. "Singing a Rodney Beecham song would be great for Camp Rock 'n' Roll," she said. "We could write about it in our next brochure. Maybe we could even make it the camp anthem."

Lark looked totally embarrassed and miserable.

"Why don't you just try out the song?" Bill suggested. "If you don't like it, we can ditch it."

Lark looked at me. "What do you think, Mary-Kate?"

"Can't hurt to see what it sounds like," I said.

Lark still didn't look sure. But she folded the note and said, "Okay. Let's give it a shot."

Stella and Bill checked out the sheet music. I could hear the girls at the door mumbling.

"Too bad my dad isn't a famous rock star," said a Corral Chick. "Then my band would come in first place."

This must be Lark's worst nightmare, I thought. I walked over to the open door. "This is a private practice," I said, then I shut the door—hard.

Janelle and I went over to Lark. She was staring at the sheet music, shaking her head. "And just how does he expect us to learn a whole new song by tomorrow?"

"We'll practice together until we do," Janelle said.

"We're not just a band—we're a team!" I said. "Like your soccer team back home."

Lark's face lit up when I said the word "soccer." For her, it was the magic word!

"Okay," Bill said. "Let's see if we can play this." From the first time we played the song, it sounded great. Lark didn't look happy, but her voice soared.

Wait till her dad sees her perform, I thought. *He'll be so proud!*

Two of a Kind Diaries

Dear Diary,

Today we really got off on the wrong foot. I say "foot" because when we woke up this morning, all of our sneakers were missing!

"It's a sneaker raid!" Janelle said as we inspected our messed-up cubbies. "Every summer one of the bunks sneaks into the other bunks to steal everyone's sneakers."

"What do they do with them?" Mary-Kate asked her.

Janelle pointed out the window. We ran to it and looked outside. Dangling from the branches of a big oak tree were dozens of sneakers—all sizes, shapes, and colors!

"Which bunk did this?" Phoebe asked.

Suddenly a song blared from the loudspeaker. It was "Material Girl."

"Bunk Madonna!" we said at the same time.

Sure enough, out by the tree, Bunk Madonna was high-fiving. And above them, dangling from one of the oak's highest branches, were my blue and yellow sneakers.

"Okay, Bunk Elvis," Mary-Kate said. "Let's show Bunk Madonna they can't mess with our blue suede shoes!" Things got goofy as we climbed the tree to get our sneakers back. Everyone was giggling and having a good time—until Erin climbed down holding a plaid sneaker.

"Phoebe, this must be yours," Erin said, holding it out. "It looks like it's from the nineteen fifties."

"Really?" Phoebe said. She lifted a berry-colored sneaker off the ground. "This must be yours. It's pink!"

Erin smiled and said, "I don't have pink sneakers. But if I did, they'd be *new*."

"You have no idea what real fashion is," Phoebe said. "You just wear the stuff your mom gives you from her magazine."

"Just because your clothes are old doesn't make them cool," Erin shot back.

I groaned, not sure how to stop their fighting. It was lucky the bell for breakfast rang.

All during breakfast I was dreading band practice. I still hadn't shown Erin the song that Phoebe and I had written.

What if Erin hates the song? I wondered. *Will Phoebe blame me if Erin refuses to sing it?*

But during band practice something amazing happened. Erin liked the song!

"The message is nice," Erin said. "And I can do some cool things on the keyboard to really make it rock." She went over to her keyboard and started to play.

Phoebe watched her from the corner of her eye. "I don't trust her, Ashley," she whispered. "How come Erin suddenly likes something I wrote? She never did before."

"I'm not taking sides, Phoebe," I said very carefully. "But try giving Erin a chance. Okay?"

Phoebe twanged a guitar string. "I'll try."

"Thanks," I said. I didn't have a clue why things were suddenly working. Maybe Erin saw that she was coming between Phoebe and me, so she decided to be extra nice. Or maybe she just liked our song.

And maybe, just maybe, I thought, *this song will help Erin and Phoebe finally hit it off and be friends!*

Chapter 11

Tuesday

Dear Diary,

Guess who came to Camp Rock 'n' Roll today? Come on, guess. Here's a hint: He came in a stretch limo, and he wore a black leather jacket and wraparound shades.

Yup—it was Rodney Beecham, rock superstar and Lark's dad!

Rodney's limo pulled into camp this morning while we were getting ready for round number two. When word got out that he was here, everyone ran to see him.

Like most celebs, Rodney wasn't alone. He came with his manager, Doris, and press agent, Lou. There were a bunch of other people, but I had no idea what they were supposed to be doing. Lou snapped a slew of pictures as Stella ran to greet Rodney.

"Stella Vickers!" Rodney shouted. He pointed to her and said, "You built this camp on rock 'n' roll, girl!"

Though I couldn't admit it to Lark, I was excited, too. Having a real rock superstar in our camp was awesome!

Rodney signed a bunch of autographs. I wanted

one, but I didn't want to act like another fan in front of Lark.

When Rodney was finished with the autographs he walked over to Lark. "How's my girl?" he asked with a thick British accent. "Singing like a little lark, no doubt!"

"Hi, Dad," Lark said.

"What brings you to camp, Rod?" Stella asked. "We didn't expect you until the taping of the special."

Doris answered. "Mr. Beecham has come to hear his daughter sing with Atomic Burger," she said.

"It was Atomic *Pizza*," Lark mumbled. "Now we're Crush."

"Suuu-per!" Rodney exclaimed.

"Mr. Beecham also wants to hear the song he wrote especially for her," Doris went on.

"And to make sure she's ready for the TV special," Rodney added. "We're calling it *Getting Mod with Rod!*"

Lark's mouth became a thin grim line.

"You picked the perfect time, Rodney," Stella said. "The girls are competing in the vocals round today."

"Vocals? As in singing?" Rodney shouted happily. "Fantastic!"

Stella put her arm around Rodney's shoulders.

"There's coffee and doughnuts in the lounge, Rodney," she said.

"Suuuuu-per!" Rodney shouted again.

Most of the kids followed Rodney and his crew to the lounge. I stayed behind with Lark.

"I wish he'd told me he was coming today," Lark said. She started biting her nails. I kind of understood why she looked so nervous. Not only did the judges have to like her singing today—so did her dad.

"Everything will be great, Lark," I said. "We're a team, remember?"

"Yeah, a team," Lark said and tried to smile.

Later, when Crush walked into the theater, Rodney was there, sitting with the judges.

Janelle interrupted my thoughts. "How do you like my new hair color?" she asked. She whipped off her hat, revealing neon purple streaks. "It's called Grape Expectations. You can use it for the next round."

"Nope," I said, shaking my head.

"Not even the tips?" Janelle asked.

Janelle, Lark, and I took our usual seats in the theater. I glanced back at Ashley. She was sitting between Erin and Phoebe. All three of them were smiling and talking to one another.

A good sign, I thought.

Stella walked to the microphone and welcomed everyone. Then she introduced Rodney. The campers went wild again as he stood up and waved.

I looked at Lark from the corner of my eye. Her hands were shaking in her lap.

I guess I'd be nervous, too, if I was singing for my dad, I thought. *And my dad isn't even a famous rock star.*

The round started with The Corral Chicks. This time they'd gotten rid of the washboard for a harpsichord.

Somewhere in the middle of their song, Rodney jumped onstage. He snatched one of the girl's Western hats and plopped it on his head. Then he began dancing a fancy two-step across the stage!

The audience loved it. They especially loved it when Rodney goofed with the judges, leading everyone in boos when Terrence gave his score.

"Your dad's a riot!" Janelle whispered to Lark.

Lark didn't answer. She stared straight ahead and squeezed the arms of her chair.

"Now we'll hear from Crush!" Stella announced.

"Go for it!" Bill whispered from the row behind us.

I gripped my drumsticks as we marched onto the stage. I set up my buckets and cans. Janelle plugged her guitar into an amp. Lark stood behind the mike.

The roadies left the stage, and the theater became quiet. Janelle played the first set of chords, and Crush began to perform.

Janelle and I started the song with the backing vocals. Then Lark came in with the lead. But as I kept the beat on my buckets, something didn't sound right. It was Lark's voice. It was shaky and off-key.

I glanced into the audience at Rodney. He had a pained look on his face as he listened to Lark.

Uh-oh, I thought. *He hates the way Lark is singing.*

I decided to do something—anything—to take Rodney's attention away from Lark. I twirled my drumsticks and tossed them up in the air. I made funny faces. I even wore one of the rubber pails on my head!

I must have looked totally outrageous, but it worked. Rodney wasn't watching Lark anymore. He was watching me.

When our song was over, Terrence spoke first. "Lark, you need to work on your delivery." He looked at me and smirked. "And Mary-Kate, try not to deliver so much!"

We got a score of seven, which was pretty good. Bill gave us a thumbs-up sign as we carried our instruments backstage. As I was stacking my gear in a corner I heard a voice say, "Well done, Mary-Kate!"

The accent was definitely British. And the only person around with a British accent was—

"Rodney Beecham!" I gasped as I spun around.

Rodney stood behind me with a big grin. "You've got it rockin' on, love," he said. "Keep up the good work!"

My mouth hung open as Rodney walked away. It stayed that way practically all day long!

Diary, I knew I liked to play the buckets and cans. But I never dreamed I'd get a thumbs-up from a famous rock star like Rodney Beecham. This had to be my *best* day ever!

Dear Diary,

This had to be my *worst* day ever!

It started out pretty well. Erin and Phoebe sat next to each other at breakfast and at lunch. Erin even gave Phoebe the tomato slices from her tuna sandwich.

"I can't believe the vocals round is today," Phoebe said. "Does everyone know the words to our song?"

Erin nodded. "Like the back of my hand."

Phoebe was dressed in pink from head to toe. She had borrowed a pink miniskirt, blouse, and shoes from the costume cabin last night. Even her lip gloss was pink!

I felt all warm and fuzzy inside. Everyone was getting along at last!

The three of us sat together in the theater, too. We all had fun watching Rodney Beecham and the other bands. Crush rocked, thanks to Mary-Kate. She was out of control on the buckets and cans. Then Gemini sang about a planet ruled by girls. A band called Knee Jerk sang about breaking up with a boyfriend.

After that, it was time for Electric Pink!

"Remember, guys," Jennifer whispered as we stood in the wings, "do your best, but don't forget to have fun!"

My heart raced as we ran onstage. Erin sat at her keyboard. Phoebe and I stood with our guitars.

"Blimey!" Rodney Beecham said, slipping on his black sunglasses. "I think I have pinkeye!"

Erin played the first few notes. Then she began to sing. I blinked. The words were totally *different*. The song wasn't about the world getting together—it was about Erin and some cute guy getting together!

What's she doing? I wondered in a panic. *I can't believe she changed the words!*

I glanced at Phoebe. She was singing through gritted teeth. We stuck to our original words as we sang backup.

Erin did *not*!

81

"'Don't forget, baby, I'll be waiting after school,'" Erin sang. "'When our hands come together, it will be so cool!'"

"'World come together, world come together,'" Phoebe and I sang. "'World come together— oooooh!'"

I was so glad when the song was over! Phoebe and I stared at Erin. She just smiled and gave us a little shrug.

"Thanks, Electric Pink," Stella said. She turned to the judges. "What was your take on that number, guys?"

I held my breath. I expected Terrence to totally trash us. Instead, he said, "Interesting. I never heard a song that compared a junior high school crush to world peace before."

"Deep, man," Rodney said, nodding. "Real deep."

I couldn't believe it when Electric Pink scored a nine. It was the highest score in the round so far!

Jennifer jumped up from her seat and cheered.

Backstage, Erin and I jumped up and down, too. Not Phoebe. She stood with her hands folded across her chest.

"Okay, Erin," Phoebe said. "What was that all about?"

"What do you mean?" Erin asked.

"As if you don't know," Phoebe said. "You

changed the words of our song without telling us!"

"Oh, that," Erin said. "I decided to tweak the words last night after everybody was asleep. I was going to tell you today, but when Rodney showed up, things got so crazy."

"He arrived this morning," Phoebe pointed out. "You had plenty of time to tell us!"

"What's the big deal?" Erin asked. Her blue eyes sparkled. "We got an awesome score, didn't we?"

"Don't just stand there, Ashley," Phoebe said. "Why don't you say something?"

What could I say but the truth?

"You really should have told us about the new words, Erin," I said. "Band members have to be on the same page."

"You see?" Phoebe said to Erin.

Then I looked at Phoebe and said, "But we did end up getting a fabulous score. So why don't we forget about it?"

"Are you telling me to forget it?" Phoebe asked.

"I said *we* should forget it."

"You meant me," Phoebe said.

Erin shook her head. She picked up her keyboard and walked back to her seat. I turned to Phoebe.

"Come on, Phoebe. Maybe you don't think it's right that Erin changed our song. And I understand that. But you've got to admit it turned out great."

Phoebe's shoulders dropped. "Don't you get it, Ashley?" she asked. "Don't you see that you totally broke your promise? You said back at school that we'd always st—"

"Ashley!" a voice cut in.

I spun around. Mary-Kate was running toward me.

"You did it, you did it!" Mary-Kate cried. "My sister got a nine score!"

"Do you believe it?" I squealed. "We just started playing and everything clicked!"

Mary-Kate and I hugged. From the corner of my eye I saw Phoebe. She was walking away with her guitar. I let go of Mary-Kate.

"Ashley?" Mary-Kate said. "What's wrong with Phoebe? She looks kind of upset."

"Phoebe's bummed out that Erin changed the words to our song," I said. "But I'm sure she'll get over it once it hits her what a great score we got."

"You're probably right," Mary-Kate said.

"Well . . . maybe I should go talk to Phoebe," I said. I turned to follow her.

"Later," Mary-Kate said as Venus took their places onstage. She grabbed my hand. "We'd better get back to our seats now."

By the time the round was over, Electric Pink was tied with Venus in overall score. Everyone headed to the rec hall for a huge pizza party. I thought I'd find Phoebe there, but I didn't.

"Doesn't this remind you of the pizza parties at school, Ashley?" Mary-Kate asked as she grabbed a slice.

I looked around the rec hall. Rodney and the instructors were jamming on their instruments while we ate five different types of pizza.

"Just the pizza part," I said. "We never had a famous rock star at school."

There was something else that was different: Phoebe wasn't there. At the White Oak pizza parties, we'd rip our slices in half so we could share toppings. We'd even eat our slices the same way by tearing off the gooey cheese first.

I glanced over at Erin. She was eating her pizza with a knife and fork. Bor-ring!

All of a sudden, I really missed Phoebe, Diary. I couldn't stop thinking about her.

"You know, Mary-Kate," I said. "Maybe I have been siding too much with Erin."

Mary-Kate's mouth was full with pizza. All she could say was, "Mmmph?"

"Maybe I was more wowed by Erin's clothes and her coolness than I thought," I went on. "And I kind of did break my promise to stick together with Phoebe."

"Mm-mmph."

"There's only one thing to do," I said with a nod. "I'm going to find Phoebe and apologize to her right now!"

Mary-Kate finally swallowed. "Go for it," she said.

I went straight to our bunk. "Are you here, Phoebe?" I called as I stepped inside.

The bunk wasn't dark yet. I could see Phoebe lying on the top bed, wrapped in her comforter. Her eyes were closed as if she was asleep—or pretending to be.

"Phoebe?" I tried again. She still didn't answer. Maybe she really was asleep.

I put the pizza down and gently nudged her shoulder. "Phoebe, it's me. I really need to talk to you."

"Mmmm," Phoebe murmured in her sleep. Then she rolled over.

"But Phoebe . . ." I tried again.

Phoebe didn't answer. I guess she really was asleep.

There's plenty of time, I told myself. *I'll straighten things out with Phoebe first thing tomorrow morning.*

And from now on, Diary, Phoebe Cahill is going to come first.

Chapter 12

Wednesday

Dear Diary,

Help! The first thing I wanted to do this morning was apologize to Phoebe. I climbed out of my bottom bunk.

"Hey, Phoebe," I started to stay. "I want to talk . . ."

I never even finished my sentence. Phoebe's paisley throws were gone. So were her sheets and comforter. Worst of all—Phoebe was gone!

"Everyone, wake up!" I shouted. "Phoebe is missing!"

Mary-Kate opened one eye. "Phoebe's cubby is empty, too," she pointed out.

Ivy came into the bunk, yawning.

"Ivy," I said, "where's Phoebe?"

"Phoebe called her mom and dad last night. She told them she didn't want to stay at camp."

My blood froze. "She . . . what?"

"They had Phoebe's aunt Marie, who lives in Philadelphia, pick her up this morning," Ivy went on. She yawned again. "Very early this morning."

"What's going to happen to our band?" Erin asked.

I glared at Erin. Was that all she could think about?

While the others washed up, I sat on my bed.

Mary-Kate sat next to me. "I don't get it," I said. "If Phoebe hated it here so much, why didn't she talk to me about it?"

"I don't know, Ashley," Mary-Kate said. "But you said you knew she was upset."

"I had no idea she was upset enough to leave!" I said. "She didn't try hard enough to let me know."

"Maybe she thought she shouldn't have to try so hard to get her best friend's attention," Mary-Kate said quietly.

I stared at my twin as she stood up and walked to her cubby. Had I been that bad a best friend?

I had to find Phoebe and talk to her fast. I quickly washed, dressed, and raced to the main office.

"Please," I begged Gloria, the camp secretary, "I have to know where Phoebe Cahill went so I can call her."

"Phoebe's new phone number is confidential," Gloria said. "It can only be given out in an emergency."

"This *is* an emergency," I said. "Our friendship is on the line!"

"Sorry," Gloria said. "Maybe she'll call you later."

I ran around the camp asking everyone where Phoebe had gone. Jennifer didn't know. Stella said the same thing Gloria did: Phoebe's phone number in Philly was top secret.

Diary, I couldn't think about music all day. Or the next choreography round. All I could think was: Did I drive my best friend away?

Dear Diary,

I've got bad news . . . and totally awesome, heel-clicking, heart-stopping, amazing news.

First, the bad news: Phoebe left camp, and Ashley feels awful. I feel awful, too. I really like Phoebe and was glad she'd come to Camp Rock 'n' Roll.

Now the good news: Right before our dance workshop, Janelle, Lark, and I were by the lake, talking.

"I'm worried about this next round," Janelle said. "I can't chew gum and play my guitar at the same time. How am I going to play my guitar and *dance* at the same time?"

"Elvis did it." I grabbed Janelle's guitar and sang as I shook my knees. "'A hunk, a hunk of burning love—'"

"Bravo!" a voice interrupted. It was Rodney's voice!

Great, I thought, turning slowly. *I just made a total jerk of myself in front of Rodney Beecham!*

Rodney was walking toward the lake. His manager

and press agent were hurrying behind him.

"You're just the girl I want to see, Mary-Jane!" Rodney said as they got closer.

"Um . . . it's Mary-Kate," I said. "But you can call me Mary-Jane if you'd like."

"Super!" Rodney laughed. He turned to his crew. "You see? I told you she was funny."

Lou and Doris laughed along. Lark didn't.

Rodney pointed his finger at me and said, "How would *you* like to perform with *me* on my TV special?"

My eyes popped wide open. *Rodney Beecham, international superstar, wants to perform with me? Me?*

"I . . . I . . . I don't get it," I stammered. "What about Lark? Isn't she supposed to sing with you?"

"Lark isn't comfortable singing in public," Rodney explained. "I saw that yesterday during the round."

Lark's eyes looked hurt. But she smiled and said, "It's okay, Mary-Kate, he told me this already. I'm cool with it."

"You're a natural performer, Mary-Kate," Rodney said. "I'd like you to play your buckets while I sing. You can sing backup, too. I'm writing the song now," he added. "It's called 'Lively Girl.'"

By now my head was spinning. Was I that Lively Girl? Was Rodney writing a song just for me?

"Rodney is catching a plane to London in two

hours," Doris said. "He needs your answer ASAP."

I opened my mouth to speak but didn't know what to say. No one had ever asked me to perform on television before.

"Do it, Mary-Kate," Janelle whispered. "You may never get this chance again."

I pictured myself singing with Rodney Beecham on national TV. I pictured all my friends watching.

"Yes!" I blurted out. "The answer is yes!"

"Suuuu-per!" Rodney exclaimed.

"I have to call my dad for permission," I said.

"He'll have to sign a release form, too," Doris said. "That gives *us* permission to show you on TV."

"I'm sure your dad will approve," Rodney said. "What father wouldn't want to see his daughter perform on TV?"

I saw Lark lower her eyes.

"We'll come back the last week of camp for the final round," the manager said. "And to tape the special."

"Then we'll roooock!" Rodney said.

Lou snapped a picture of me. Rodney gave Lark a hug. Then they and Doris hurried up the hill to the waiting limo.

"Thank you!" I called after them. I turned to Janelle and Lark and squealed, "I can't belieeeeve it! Ohmigosh! I have to tell Ashley!"

Chapter 13

Thursday

Dear Diary,

Since yesterday I've had Phoebe on the brain. I can't stop thinking about how to reach her!

I tried calling Phoebe's mom and dad in San Francisco, but I kept getting their answering machine.

Are they on their way to Philadelphia to bring Phoebe home? I wondered. *I hope not!*

I tried e-mailing Phoebe from the camp office, but she never e-mailed me back.

"It's all my fault," I told Mary-Kate at breakfast. "I never should have put Erin before Phoebe!"

Mary-Kate stared at me, starry-eyed. "I can't believe it, Ashley," she said. "I'm going to sing on TV. Me!"

I smiled at my sister. Her head was still in the clouds and that was okay. I am happy for her. But unhappy for Phoebe—and me.

Band practice later just made it worse. . . .

"Now that Phoebe left," Jennifer told Erin and me, "the two of you will have to perform as a duet."

"A duet?" I repeated. It sounded so final. As though Phoebe wasn't coming back!

"That's so cool." Erin squealed. "Just you and me—right, Ashley? Maybe we can wear the exact same outfits! And call ourselves Electric Pink Times 2!"

I whirled to face Erin. "It's not cool," I told her. "Phoebe is my best friend!"

Maybe I did overreact, Diary. But at that moment I also made up my mind.

I'm going to find Phoebe and get her to come back to Camp Rock 'n' Roll. No matter what it takes!

Dear Diary,

Just when I thought everything was perfect, I found out something that really reeked!

At the end of the day my bunk mates decided to celebrate my good news. So instead of going to the mess hall for dinner, Ivy ordered two pizzas. We brought in a boom box and blasted all kinds of music—rap, rock, even a few oldies from the fifties. Hey, this is Bunk Elvis!

But Ashley wasn't in the mood to celebrate with us. She was still hurting over Phoebe. Lark was acting gloomy, too. She had been like that ever since her dad left. After we finished the pizza, Janelle made a toast with a can of orange soda. "To Mary-Kate, the future Queen of Rock!" she declared. "May she remember us when she's at the top . . . and when we all want tickets to major rock concerts!"

Everyone clapped and whistled. Only Lark didn't join in. She stood up, excused herself, and left the bunk.

"Is it something I said?" Janelle asked.

"Probably not," I said, standing up. "I'll find out what's bothering her."

I left Bunk Elvis to look for Lark. She was exactly where I thought I'd find her: on the playing field, bouncing a soccer ball on one knee.

"Shoot it here!" I called.

Lark kicked the ball over to me, and I kicked it back. We didn't say a word as we kicked the ball back and forth. Finally I had to speak up.

"What's up, Lark?" I asked. "You've been acting kind of weird ever since your dad left yesterday."

Lark put her foot on top of the ball to keep it from rolling. I could see her chin quivering.

"I *don't* like singing in public," she said. "But I still wanted my dad to be proud of me. That's why I was so nervous in the vocals round."

"I figured that," I said, nodding.

"Then he asked you to be in the TV special

instead of me," Lark said. "He made me feel like such a loser."

"But," I said slowly, "when your dad asked me, you said it was okay."

"What else could I say?" Lark asked. "My dad has no idea how bad he made me feel."

I'd had no idea how Lark really felt, either. And it made me feel horrible!

"Listen, I won't do the special," I told her. "You're a much better singer than I am, anyway."

Lark shook her head. "You're the better performer," she said. "And that's what Dad wants."

"How can I do the special?" I asked. "Look how upset you are!"

"I'll deal with it." Lark looked me straight in the eye. "Just promise me you'll do the special, Mary-Kate."

I noticed the studded bracelet around Lark's wrist. It was the friendship bracelet I had given her in arts and crafts.

How could I do this to my new friend? How could I come between her and her dad?

"No way, Lark," I said, shaking my head.

"Do it, Mary-Kate," Lark insisted. "If you don't, my dad will know how upset I am. He'll think I'm a big baby."

Lark wasn't crying anymore. The look on her

face told me she was serious. "If you're my friend," she said, "you'll promise me."

"Okay," I said slowly. "I promise."

"Good." Lark sniffed. She wiped her face with the sleeve of her red hoodie. "We'd better get back to the bunk before they come looking for us."

"Yeah," I said, forcing a smile.

We left the ball on the field and headed back to Bunk Elvis. Lark started chatting about her favorite soccer players. I hardly heard her, because all I could think about was the TV special.

It's not right, I thought. *Rodney Beecham shouldn't be performing with me—he should be performing with his daughter. He should be performing with Lark!*

I gazed at the sun going down behind the trees.

Then again, I thought, *this is my chance to be on TV with a rock superstar!*

Diary, what would you do if you were me?

Would you pick friendship?

Or *fame*?

TO BE CONTINUED

in

TWO OF A KIND: *Twist and Shout*

#36 Twist and Shout

Dear Diary,

Today Phoebe, Erin, and I carried our new sixties outfits from the costume cabin to the music building. Then we headed to the mess hall for lunch. Our bunk counselor Ivy sat across from me. Instead of eating spaghetti and meatballs like the rest of us, she just nibbled on a roll.

"What's up, Ivy?" I asked. "Don't you feel well?"

"I have no appetite," Ivy said. "The girls from Venus left awesome cookies in the counselors' lounge today."

Venus? I looked sideways at Phoebe and Erin.

"Those girls should win an award for the nicest band," Ivy said. "Don't you think?"

I glanced over at the next table. Abigail was winding spaghetti on a fork. She looked right at me and smirked. Then Skye speared a meatball and waved it at me.

"Why is she doing that?" Phoebe whispered.

"Let's just ignore them," I whispered.

After lunch we all headed to the music building for

band practice. We kicked off our sneakers and stuck our feet into our awesome go-go boots.

Squish!

"Ewww!" Phoebe cried.

We yanked our boots off and gasped. Our feet were covered with red and brown goop. When we tipped our boots over, clumps of spaghetti and meatballs plopped out on the floor.

"Gross!" I cried.

"Who would do this to our vintage go-go boots? Now they're totally ruined!" Phoebe wailed.

I remembered the look Abigail gave me in the mess hall. And that meatball Skye waved at me. I had a pretty good idea who had ruined our boots

But Erin spoke up before I did.

"The girls from Venus have been acting pretty snooty lately," Erin said. "It must have been them."

"We can't let Venus get away with this," Phoebe said. "We have to tell Stella."

"We're Electric Pink—not Electric Rat-Fink," I argued. "And we don't have any proof that Venus did it."

"Proof-shmoof." Erin narrowed her blue eyes. "We should get even. A prank for a prank, that's what I say!"

I knew the Battle of the Bands would be tough, Diary. But I never dreamed it would be all-out war!

WIN A SUPER COOL ELECTRIC GUITAR!

One Grand Prize Winner will receive a *FENDER* Electric Guitar

Two Of A Kind
Electric Guitar Sweepstakes
OFFICIAL RULES:

1. No purchase or payment necessary to enter or win.

2. How to Enter. To enter, complete the official entry form or hand print your name, address, age, and phone number along with the words "*Two Of A Kind* Electric Guitar Sweepstakes" on a 3" x 5" card and mail to: *Two Of A Kind* Electric Guitar Sweepstakes, c/o HarperEntertainment, Attn: Children's Marketing Department, 10 East 53rd Street, New York, NY 10022. Entries must be received no later than October 30, 2004. Enter as often as you wish, but each entry must be mailed separately. One entry per envelope. Partially completed, illegible, or mechanically reproduced entries will not be accepted. Sponsor are not responsible for lost, late, mutilated, illegible, stolen, postage due, incomplete, or misdirected entries. All entries become the property of Dualstar Entertainment Group, LLC, and will not be returned.

3. Eligibility. Sweepstakes open to all legal residents of the United States (excluding Colorado and Rhode Island), who are between the ages of five and fifteen on October 30, 2004 excluding employees and immediate family members of HarperCollins Publishers, Inc., ("HarperCollins"), Warner Bros.Pictures Inc. ("Warner"), Parachute Properties and Parachute Press, Inc., and their respective subsidiaries and affiliates, officers, directors, shareholders, employees, agents, attorneys, and other representatives and their immediate families (individually and collectively, 'Parachute'), Dualstar Entertainment Group, LLC, and its subsidiaries and affiliates, officers, directors, shareholders, employees, agents, attorneys, and other representatives and their immediate families (individually and collectively, "Dualstar"), and their respective parent companies, affiliates, subsidiaries, advertising, promotion and fulfillment agencies, and the persons with whom each of the above are domiciled. All applicable federal, state and local laws and regulations apply. Offer void where prohibited or restricted by law.

4. Odds of Winning. Odds of winning depend on the total number of entries received. Approximately 300,000 sweepstakes announcements published. All prizes will be awarded. Winners will be randomly drawn on or about November 15, 2004, by HarperCollins, whose decision is final. Potential winners will be notified by mail and will be required to sign and return an affidavit of eligibility and release of liability within 14 days of notification. Prizes won by minors will be awarded to parent or legal guardian who must sign and return all required legal documents. By acceptance of their prize, winners consent to the use of their names, photographs, likeness, and biographical information by HarperCollins, Parachute, Dualstar, and for publicity purposes without further compensation except where prohibited.

5. Grand Prize. One Grand Prize Winner will win a Fender electric guitar. Approximate retail value of prize totals $300.00.

6. Prize Limitations. All prizes will be awarded. Only one prize will be awarded per individual, family, or household. Prizes are non-transferable and cannot be sold or redeemed for cash. No cash substitute is available. Any federal, state, or local taxes are the responsibility of the winner. Sponsor may substitute prize of equal or greater value, if necessary, due to availability.

7. Additional terms: By participating, entrants agree a) to the official rules and decisions of the judges, which will be final in all respects; and to waive any claim to ambiguity of the official rules and b) to release, discharge, and hold harmless HarperCollins, Warner, Parachute, Dualstar, and their respective parent companies, affiliates, subsidiaries, employees and representatives and advertising, promotion and fulfillment agencies from and against any and all liability or damages associated with acceptance, use, or misuse of any prize received or participation in any sweepstakes-related activity or participation in this Sweepstakes.

8. Dispute Resolution. Any dispute arising from this Sweepstakes will be determined according to the laws of the State of New York, without reference to its conflict of law principles, and the entrants consent to the personal jurisdiction of the State and Federal courts located in New York County and agree that such courts have exclusive jurisdiction over all such disputes.

9. Winner Information. To obtain the name of the winner, please send your request and a self-addressed stamped envelope (residents of Vermont may omit return postage) to *Two Of A Kind* Electric Guitar Winner, c/o HarperEntertainment, 10 East 53rd Street, New York, NY 10022 by December 15, 2005.

10. Sweepstakes Sponsor: HarperCollins Publishers, Inc. Fender© Musical Instruments Corporation is not affiliated, connected or associated with this Sweepstakes in any manner and bears no responsibility for the administration of this Sweepstakes.

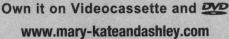

mary-kate olsen
ashley olsen
eugene levy
R
new york minute
In Theaters May 7th
www.newyorkminutemovie.com
WARNER BROS. PICTURES